Suzie-Que and Pepperanne

"The Mouseguest"

Book 1

in the tales of

Suzie-Que and Pepperanne

S.F. Heskin

For Pepper

My furry, little soulmate.

XOX

"The Mouseguest"

Pepperanne, my friend the cat,
keeps an eye on where I'm at.
I'm hardly walking out the door,
when she's between my foot and floor.

I careful tred about the house,
Lest she be in pursuit of mouse.
For then, no telling where she'll be,
and I may end on face and knee!

She prowls about our humble home,
to make sure we are quite alone;
and when "All's Clear!" is safe to vouch,
she'll cozy up upon the couch.

We then sit down to tea and sweets,
and other yummy, feline treats.
Oh, how I love to sit and chat,
with Pepperanne, my friend the cat.

One day, while chatting over tea,
a queer event distracted me.
There stood a mouse three inches tall,
awaiting in the kitchen hall.

"May we help you?" I asked annoyed.
While with his tail he crudely toyed.
"Just moving in to my new house."
Replied this rude and cheeky mouse.

Then from my plate a spoon he stole,
and disappeared down a small hole.
That crazy mouse was not too shrewd.
He clearly thought my spoon was food.

Well now he's sealed his certain doom.
within my house I'll make no room;
for though our meeting was quite brief,
he revealed himself to be a thief.

Sometimes, in morning when I wake,
I find my head does slightly ache;
and find when further I inspect,
my hair is shorter, I suspect.

It seems that cheeky mouse at night,
decides he's hungry for a bite;
and since he's feeble in the eyes,
and also not what you'd call wise ...

He sets to feasting on my hair;
believing that it's Camembert!
What shall I do? I am appalled.
In time, I'll be completely bald!

Oh, Pepperanne!
Do help me please!
Explain to him,
MY HAIR IS NOT CHEESE!

Pepperanne and I have thought.
To this mouse, a lesson must be taught.
We have a plan with which to scare,
so he shall leave to live elsewhere.

We'll don armor, like valiant nights,
who dressed as such for their brave fights;
and with our battle arms in air,
we'll challenge him, "Fight if you DARE!"

He'll soon be off to pack his bags,
and we shall raise our victory flags.
Then peace shall reign throughout our house,
without that crazy, cheeky mouse.

It seems we took our plan too far.
The outcome was a bit bizarre.
Our goal was just to scare the mouse;
not cause such panic in the house.

That silly mouse ran to and fro,
which way to turn he didn't know.
Instead of running up the hall,
he ran top speed into the wall.

Then quickly rising from the floor,
he ran into a cabinet door;
then spun around with feet in air,
and ran into a kitchen chair.

Oh what a scene this mouse did cause;
it seems he can't control his paws.
There's something which is not quite right.
Perhaps it is his failing sight.

We now have come to the decision,
this mouse is quite impaired of vision.
He doesn't mean to cause insult.
His blindness makes him difficult.

"It's such a nuisance night and day,
to labour, just to find one's way."
Our mouse confessed through sobbing tears.
"I haven't seen clearly in years!"

While Pepperanne and I conversed,
our opinion of this mouse reversed.
At once together we agreed,
a pair of glasses was in need.

So to the mouse we gave this gift;
at which he first cautiously sniffed;
and then put on and beamed with glee;
"At last, I can precisely see!"

These days at tea we often jest,
of how we met our dear new guest.
And to the menu of our tea,
we've added cheddar, swiss and brie.

My hair has grown to it's full length,
as our bonds of friendship grow in strength.
All is forgiven, all is well,
In bliss and peace we all do dwell.

And though its nice to make new friends;
I cherish that when each day ends;
I say good night with a pet-and-pat;
to my best friend Pepperanne the cat.

THE END

Suzie-Que and Pepperanne

Stay tuned for

Book 2

"What's in a Name?"

Book 2

in the tales of

Suzie-Que and Pepperanne

https://www.facebook.com/PepperannesPage

S.F. Heskin

Born and raised in New York City, S.F. Heskin is an illustrator, writer and graphic designer. The Suzie-Que and Pepperanne series was inspired by her 20 year relationship with an extraordinary cat named Pepper. That relationship continues to be an inspiration to her, as all true friendships do.

She attended Parsons School of Design in New York City where she received her Bachelor of Arts in Design and Management. In 2009 she received her Masters of Art in Illustration from the Fashion Institute of Technology, also in New York.

Today she works as a V.P. of Graphic Production at a leading corporate firm, and continues to pursue her deepest passion, writing and illustrating children's books. Her work has been featured in the SCBWI Bulletin and took first-place honors at the JP Morgan Chase Corporate Challenge T-shirt design competition (Winner 2006 and 2009).

Coming Soon

February 2014

Pepper Mill Publications

An online shop for all your
Suzie-Que and Pepperanne desires.
Offering greeting cards, books, and handmade gifts,
Pepper Mill Publications will offer unique
items for every occasion.

"Season your Greetings with a Dash of Pepper!"

www.peppermillpublications.com

www.ingramcontent.com/pod-product-compliance
Lightning Source LLC
Chambersburg PA
CBHW041032170626
46815CB00001B/60